For Gavin and Violet

ALADDIN

An imprint of Simon & Schuster Children's Publishing Division
1230 Avenue of the Americas, New York, New York 10020
First Aladdin hardcover edition April 2019
Copyright © 2019 by Chad J. Thompson
All rights reserved, including the right of reproduction in whole or in part in any form.
ALADDIN and related logo are registered trademarks of Simon & Schuster, Inc.
For information about special discounts for bulk purchases, please contact Simon & Schuster Special Sales
at 1-866-506-1949 or business@simonandschuster.com.
The Simon & Schuster Speakers Bureau can bring authors to your live event. For more information or
to book an event contact the Simon & Schuster Speakers Bureau at
1-866-248-3049 or visit our website at www.simonspeakers.com.
Series designed by Karina Granda
Book designed by Tiara Iandiorio
The illustrations for this book were rendered digitally.
The text of this book was set in Bliss and Candy Square.
Manufactured in China 0219 SCP
2 4 6 8 10 9 7 5 3 1
Library of Congress Control Number 2018955241
ISBN 978-1-4814-7097-1 (hc)
ISBN 978-1-4814-7098-8 (eBook)

Rhymes
with
Claire

written and illustrated by
CHAD J. THOMPSON

ALADDIN   New York   London   Toronto   Sydney   New Delhi

What was I thinking?

I've got to get to school fast and warn Claire!

CLAIRE!

Claire! . . . Last night . . .

I put a box in your driveway . . .

Don't open . . . Magic bird . . . He's

BIG TROUBLE . . .

Aaahhh! Why are you a slug?

What's going on, Doug?

You've got to get out of here! RUN, CLAIRE!

CLAIRE HARE!

A *fair*? What happened to Mr. Nethery's class?

We *should* be in math class, but . . .

As long as we're here . . .

CLAIRE CHAIR.

Wow! Look how high up we are!

I can see my house! And, look, there's our school.

Two bears?
Knock it
off, Otto.

POP!

Gosh, he's
heavy.

Hey, get back here!

They're headed for
the Tilt-A-Whirl.

Gotcha!

Mine is falling asleep.

This one is already snoozing. Now what?

CLAIRE LAIR!

Let's just put them near that big bear . . .

and then we'll go.

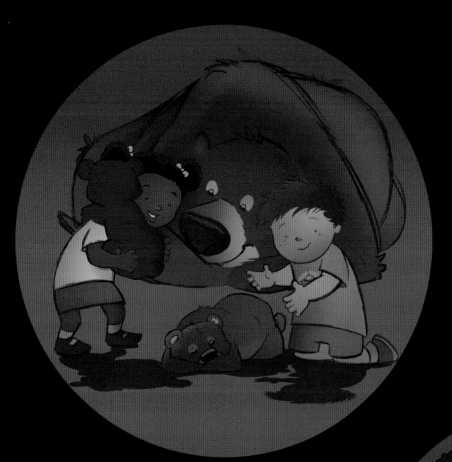

Nighty night, boys.

Here's Mommy.

Now, how do we
get out of here?

Great idea, Otto.

Now let's get back to school.

Can I give your magic bird a try?

Heeeyyy . . . !